GREAT ILLUSTRATED CLASSICS

HANS BRINKER

Mary Mapes Dodge

adapted by
Malvina G. Vogel

**Illustrations by
Floris Freshman**

BARONET BOOKS, New York, New York

Contents

About the Author

When Mary Elizabeth Mapes was born in New York City in 1831, she lived with a Dutch grandmother in a city with traces of New Amsterdam's Dutch settlers from the 1600s.

Lizzie came from a wealthy family and her father and his many writer friends taught her to love books. Her husband, William Dodge, continued encouraging her. An 1855 business trip took Dodge to Holland, and the books he brought back about the country and its people captivated Lizzie.

When Dodge left her and their two young sons, Lizzie had to work to support them. She began writing, starting with articles about strong-minded, independent women who had made a place for themselves in American history.

In 1865, Mary Mapes Dodge published her first novel for children, *Hans Brinker, or the*

Silver Skates. Because the book is so accurate in describing Holland's history, geography, culture, and people, readers are always amazed to learn that Lizzie had never visited there before she wrote about it. That visit to Holland, her lifelong dream, was finally made seven years after *Hans Brinker* was published!

Next came a magazine for children, *St. Nicholas*, which Lizzie Dodge created in 1873 and edited until her death in 1905. During that time, the finest children's authors wrote for it, including Rudyard Kipling, Mark Twain, Louisa May Alcott, Henry Wadsworth Longfellow, and Robert Louis Stevenson.

Children and adults have read and loved *Hans Brinker* for over 100 years. When today's readers hear skates scraping the ice or watch a Winter Olympics, they are sure to have fond memories of Hans, Gretel, and the children of Broek racing for the Silver Skates!

They Didn't Pay Much Attention to the Cold.

Chapter 1

The Poor Brinker Family

Long ago, in the 1840's, on a cold but bright December morning, two children were kneeling on the bank of a frozen canal in Holland. Ice covered that country's canals all winter long, and skating was the main means of transportation.

The children's thin jackets barely warmed their shivering bodies, but fifteen-year-old Hans Brinker and his twelve-year-old sister, Gretel, didn't pay much attention to the cold, as their numb red fingers tried to fasten "things" onto their feet.

Those strange-looking "things" were clumsy pieces of wood which Hans had carved into runners. They were pierced with holes into which he threaded strips of rawhide, which tied around their shoes and feet. These took the place of regular ice skates, which their poor peasant mother couldn't afford to buy for them, but which still managed to give Hans and Gretel many happy hours on the ice.

"Come on, Gretel," called Hans as he stood up and glided smoothly across the canal, avoiding the peasant women on their way to market and the young men on their way to work.

"I can't, Hans," groaned his sister. "My right foot still hurts from where the string cut it the last time I wore the skates."

"Then tie them higher," said her brother, intent on the circles he was making on the ice.

"I can't! The string is too short!"

"Troublesome girls!" he muttered, throwing his arms up in the air, but skating towards his

"Come On, Gretel," Called Hans.

sister anyway. "You really should have worn your heavy leather shoes, Gretel."

"Oh, Hans, have you forgotten? Father threw them in the fire." And tears began trickling down Gretel's cheeks.

Hans knelt beside his sister. "I'll fix it," he said gently as he took off his cap and tore out its ragged lining. He folded it over and made a pad of it, then adjusted it over the top of Gretel's worn-out shoe and wound the strings around her foot. "We'd better hurry though. Mother will be needing us soon."

In another moment, the two were laughing, as hand in hand they flew along the frozen canal. But within moments, Hans's smooth glides turned into squeaky jerks and he finally lay sprawled on the ice.

"Are you hurt, Hans?" called Gretel. "No, of course not, not when you laugh with your feet kicking the air!"

No sooner had she darted away than Hans was on his feet again, chasing her until her

Sprawled on the Ice

skates, too, began to squeak and jerk. Just as she was about to fall and Hans was reaching out to catch her, they heard their mother calling them.

As hard as it was to interrupt their few minutes of fun, Hans and Gretel quickly pulled off their skates and headed toward their parents' cottage, not far from the edge of the canal.

With land so flat in Holland, everything from tall to small could be seen clearly, no matter how far away it was. Only long dikes interrupted that flatness. These walls of dirt had been built to keep the sea, the rivers, the lakes, and canals from flooding the land. Some dikes were so big that roads, houses, and shops were built on them.

Sometimes, however, those dikes sprang leaks or even caved in because of the great pressure of the water against them. Then the rushing water would bury entire towns and villages, killing everyone in its path. Therefore, a careful watch was kept on the dikes

They Heard Their Mother Calling.

night and day. When a leak *was* discovered, all the townspeople would rush to shore up the dikes by pressing straw mats, strengthened with clay and stone, against them.

Meitje Brinker, standing in the doorway of her cottage waiting for her children, knew just how dangerous working on these dikes could be. Her husband, Raff, had worked on the dikes until his accident ten years ago. During a terrible sleet storm, he had fallen from the dike's scaffolding and was carried home, unconscious.

From that day on, Raff Brinker never worked again. His mind and his memory were gone. He made sounds, but couldn't speak. His eyes moved, but only stared into space. He had the strength of a giant, but the intelligence of a baby. Because of that, Mrs. Brinker had to be with him constantly, to control him or care for him.

Both Mrs. Brinker and Hans had wonderful memories of the once cheerful, hearty man

Meitje Brinker

who loved carrying his son on his strong shoulders. Gretel was only a baby when the accident happened and knew her father only as the strange, silent man who sometimes did terrible things, like throwing her shoes into the fire for no reason!

Mrs. Brinker barely managed to support her family by raising vegetables, spinning, and knitting. She had even worked on the canal barges and at times harnessed herself to the tow ropes with other women to pull the canal boats from shore.

Once Hans was old enough, he insisted that he take over this work, since his mother was needed more and more at home as his father became more and more helpless. He and Gretel also did household chores, like gathering peat—clumps of moss and rotted plants—and storing it to burn as fuel in their fireplace. Hans also rode towing-horses on the canal, while Gretel tended geese for some of the local farmers.

She Even Worked on the Barges.

HANS BRINKER

Hans was very skilled at carving. He was also at the top of his class at school, when he could go, much to the dismay of many of the other boys who preferred to sneer at him because of his patched clothes.

Gretel hated to learn her lessons at school but loved to sing. She had a sweet voice and often sang to cheer her mother as she worked at spinning or knitting or baking.

The children were able to attend school only occasionally because they had to take care of their father while their mother was out of the cottage working. For the past month, that was why they had been kept home.

Now they hurried off the ice toward their cottage. They knew that their mother had bread to bake and knitting to finish, all to be taken to market to earn the little family's needs.

Gretel Loved to Sing.

Skating Down the Canal

Chapter 2

Two Good-Hearted Friends

While Hans and Gretel were busy helping their mother on this cold December morning, a happy group of teenage boys and girls came skating down the canal. They were dressed so colorfully that they looked like a bed of tulips blown along by the wind.

Among the girls and boys on the ice were Hilda van Gleck, the daughter of the rich mayor of the town; Annie Bouman, a pretty peasant girl; Rychie Korbes, the pompous daughter of an important official in the city of Amsterdam; Katrinka Flack, a pretty but flighty teenager; Carl Schummel, the obnoxious son of a wealthy businessman; wealthy, generous, and well-brought-up Peter van Holp and his younger brother Ludwig; Lambert van Mounen, a polite and intelligent boy; and Jacob Poot, a chubby, easygoing lad who good-naturedly took much teasing from his friends.

All were racing along, sometimes dodging in and out of those grownups skating leisurely towards town or working-people hurrying to their shops or women heading to market, balancing their wares on their heads.

The skating didn't stop the young people from talking excitedly about the great skating race Hilda van Gleck was planning as part of her mother's birthday celebration. "They're going to give a wonderful prize for the best skaters—a pair of magnificent Silver Skates," announced Rychie Korbes, who always knew everything. "The girls' skates will have silver bells on them, and the boys' will have an engraved arrow."

On the Canal

"Who's entering the race?" asked Katrinka.

"Why, all of us, of course!" said Rychie. "You must join in. We've got to get to school now. We'll talk about it at noon."

Just as they had planned, the boys and girls met for an hour of skating at recess.

Carl Schummel had been skating alongside Hilda von Gleck when he pointed to Hans and Gretel at the edge of the canal and said mockingly, "There's a pair of ragpickers coming on the ice, with skates that must have been a gift from the king!" He laughed at his cruel joke, though no one else did.

"They are kind but poor peasant children," said Hilda gently. "It must have been hard for them to learn to skate on such strange skates. The boy probably made them himself."

Hilda skated off toward the two children and stopped beside Gretel. "You look very cold today, Gretel," said Hilda with genuine concern. "You should wear a warmer jacket."

Gretel, who had nothing else to wear, tried

"Ragpickers!"

to laugh, but felt the tears welling up in her eyes. "I-I'm not really cold," she stammered. "Besides, I'll warm up when I skate. Please don't bother yourself about me, my lady."

Hans, who was standing nearby, saw his sister's sadness and said, "My sister hasn't complained of the cold, but I do agree this is bitter weather."

Hilda was angry at herself. "Please forgive me! That was a stupid thing to say! I didn't mean any harm; I was only concerned about Gretel. But listen, I came by to ask you both to join the grand race for my mother's birthday. There's no fee to enter, and the prizes are wonderful Silver Skates."

Hans tipped his cap and answered respectfully, "Thank you, miss. But even if we did enter, our skates wouldn't last for a race. They're made of wood and once they get damp, they stick and trip us. But we would really like to come to the race and watch."

"Certainly," said Hilda, looking kindly at the

"I-I'm Not Really Cold."

two eager faces and wishing that she hadn't spent most of her allowance on silly things. She had eight *kwartjes* left, enough to pay for one pair of skates. "Decide between yourselves which of you is the better skater and has the better chance of winning the race. Buy skates for that one." With that, she dropped the eight pieces of silver into the hand of a startled Hans and swiftly skated away to join her friends.

"Miss van Gleck!" called Hans, stumbling after her. "We can't take this money, though we appreciate your kindness."

"Why not?" she asked in amazement.

"Because we haven't earned it."

Hilda was a very bright, quick girl. She had noticed Gretel wearing a pretty wooden chain on her neck and immediately got an idea. "Carve a chain for me, Hans, like the one you made for your sister. That way, you will have earned the money."

"I will, miss. I'll work all night. By tomor-

"Buy Skates for that One."

row, you'll have the finest wood necklace I can make!" But Hans was talking to Hilda's back, for she had already skated off, leaving him stunned as he gazed after her.

"What a wonderful lady!" gasped Gretel. "We're so lucky. If mother sends us to the marketplace in Amsterdam tomorrow, you'll be able to buy yourself the skates."

"Since *I'm* earning the money, I'll decide how to spend it," insisted Hans. "And I'll spend it for some wool cloth so you can have a warm jacket, Gretel."

"Not buy yourself the skates?" cried Gretel in dismay. "But you must! Besides, I'm not cold that often, really I'm not!"

Hans looked down at the money in his hand. Never in his life had he longed for a pair of skates as he did now. Never had he wished to test his skating against the other boys. Never had he felt so certain that with a good pair of steel runners, he could keep up with or outdistance them in the race.

"The Finest Necklace I Can Make!"

But on the other hand, he knew that with a week's practice on good runners, Gretel could be a better skater than either Rychie or Katrinka.

That made up Hans's mind. "If you won't have a warm jacket," he told his sister, "you'll have the skates."

"But Hilda gave the money to *you*, Hans!"

Hans shook his head and turned toward their cottage. His mind was made up, and he was eager to share the good news with his mother. Gretel had no choice but to follow him home.

By late afternoon of the following day, a proud and happy Hans Brinker watched his sister fly in and out among the crowds of skaters on the canal. Not only was Gretel enjoying her new skates, but she was wearing a warm red jacket that kind-hearted Hilda had given her. Admiring people, both old and young, couldn't take their eyes off Gretel.

"Look at that!" exclaimed Peter van Holp to

"You'll Have the Skates."

Carl Schummel. "That little girl in the red jacket and patched skirt skates as if she has toes on her heels and eyes in back of her head! Won't it be something if she enters the race and beats Katrinka!"

"Shh! Not so loud!" sneered Carl. "That girl in rags is Hilda's special pet. I hear Hilda bought her those skates as a gift."

"Good! Good!" exclaimed Peter smiling, for Hilda was his best friend. "Hilda is always doing good for other people." And he sped off on the ice, cutting a double 8, as he glided up beside Hilda.

The two young people skated hand in hand, laughing and talking in whispers. So it wasn't that surprising Peter decided that his sister needed a wooden necklace just like Hilda's and that Hans Brinker was the only one skilled enough to carve exactly what he wanted!

Cutting a Double 8

Sitting Limply

Chapter 3

Ten-Year-Old Mysteries

Mrs. Brinker shared her children's joy at Gretel's new skates and at the money Hans had earned by making the second wooden necklace. "I'm happy that you'll both have real skates now," she told them.

"Why, look at father! He looks happy too!" exclaimed Gretel.

Mrs. Brinker turned to her husband seated limply in a chair. The glimmer of hope in her eyes died away as she saw the dull stare with which he looked at everything. "No, no," she sighed. "He doesn't know or understand anything. . . Now, are you two ready to leave for Amsterdam to get Hans's skates?"

"Mother, you need so many things more than I need skates," argued Hans. "A new treadle for your spinning wheel, wool, food, and—"

"Now listen, Hans. Your eight pieces of silver can't buy everything we need. Ah, if only our stolen money could be returned, our lives would be so much better. There's been no sign of it since the day before your dear father's accident ten years ago. And what's even stranger, my old stone pot has been missing since then as well, though I can't understand why a thief would take *that*!"

"Yet we've torn the cottage apart searching for the money, mother," said Hans. "Do you think father knows anything about it?"

"He probably does, but he has no way of telling us. Maybe he used the money to pay for the mysterious silver watch we've been guarding since that day. . . No, no, I can't believe he'd

"Eight Pieces of Silver Can't Buy Everything."

use our life savings for that. He was too shrewd and too careful with our thousand guilders to spend it on a watch that isn't worth a quarter of that amount!"

"Then where *did* the watch come from?"

Mrs. Brinker looked sadly toward her husband, who was staring blankly at the floor. "I'm afraid we'll never know that, Hans. I tried showing him the watch many times, but he doesn't react to seeing it any more than he does to seeing a potato."

"And when he gave it to you that terrible stormy night, didn't he tell you anything about where it came from?"

"He only said to take good care of it until he asked for it again. Then, just as he was about to say more, one of his fellow-workers rushed in, crying, 'Come, Raff! The water's rising and the dike's in danger! We need you!' Your brave father grabbed his tools and ran out. That was the last I saw of him in his right mind."

Hans had heard the story of his father's ac-

Mrs. Brinker Looked Sadly at Her Husband.

cident over and over, but he seemed to sense his mother's need to repeat it now.

"When they brought him in around midnight, his head was cut and bruised," she went on. "He was nearly dead. His fever lasted a long time, but eventually went away. However, his dullness stayed and got worse and worse."

Hans had seen his mother take the watch from its hiding-place in times of great need. He knew she had been trying to decide whether or not to sell it. And each time, she would say, "No, we must be almost starving before I betray your father's trust."

"You've been very brave to keep it for so long, mother, and very loyal to father."

"What I don't understand is why a thief would come here to steal from *us*. We weren't rich folks; we worked hard for every guilder we managed to save. We put each coin into a pouch and when the pouch was filled, we used an old sock for the next one. And it wasn't only copper and silver; we had some gold too. That

"We Must Be Almost Starving."

money was to provide a good education for you and Gretel, and to make your father and me comfortable in our old age.

"Last winter, when you and Gretel were delirious with high fever and our food was nearly gone, I tried asking him, 'Where's the money, Raff? Who has it?' He whispered gibberish back to me. I even tried screaming at him, but that didn't help. I might as well have been talking to a stone.

"But enough talk about that money. Right now, it's more important for you to start for the market-place in Amsterdam."

"Mother, while I'd love to have those skates, I'd rather use my money to bring a doctor from Amsterdam to see father."

"A doctor wouldn't come for twice that amount! And it wouldn't do any good if he did. You don't know what I've already spent for doctors. Nothing helped. Now go, Hans. It's five miles to Amsterdam. Go before it gets too late. Go and buy your skates!"

"A Doctor to See Father"

The Great Dr. Boekman

Chapter 4

An Unexpected Meeting

The ice on the canal was perfect for skating, but the wooden runners on Hans's skates squeaked as he scraped along.

As he was crossing over to the opposite fork of the canal, Hans was startled to see skating towards him the great Dr. Gerard Boekman, the most famous physician and surgeon in Holland. Hans had never met the man, but had seem pictures of him in many shop windows in Amsterdam.

Dr. Boekman was a tall, thin man whose stern blue eyes and tight, downturned lips seemed to say "Don't smile at me and don't talk to me unless I give you permission!"

But the voice of Hans Brinker's conscience said to him, "Here comes the greatest doctor in the whole world. You have no right to buy skates with money that could pay him to help your father! You must talk to him!"

Hans's heart rose up to his throat, but he found his voice long enough to call out, "Dr. Boekman!"

The great man halted and looked around him with a scowl.

"I'm in for it now!" thought Hans as he skated closer to the fierce-looking doctor. Then aloud he said, "Dr. Boekman, I have to ask you a great favor."

"Humph!" muttered the doctor. "I've no money for beggars. Get out of my way!" And he started to skate off.

"I'm no beggar, sir," said Hans as he held his silver coins out to the man. "I wish to consult with you about my father. He's a living man,

Hans Skated Closer.

but sits and acts like a dead one. He can't think. His words mean nothing. But he's not sick. He fell off the dike."

The doctor listened as Hans told the whole story, jumping from one thought to another, jumbling the details, finding himself unable to stop the tears from flowing. He finally ended his story with the plea: ""Oh, please see him, Doctor. His body is well, but his mind is sick. I know this isn't much money, but take it. I'll earn more. I'll work for you for the rest of my life if only you'll cure my father!"

The doctor's face seemed to undergo a remarkable change. His eyes became soft and even moist. The hand that had clutched a cane as if to strike a beggar was now gently holding the boy's shoulder. "Put away your money, my boy," he said. "I don't want it. I will see your father, but from what you've told me of the last ten years, I fear this is a hopeless case. I'm on my way to Leyden now, but I expect to return in a week. I'll see your father then."

Unable to Stop the Tears

"Thank you, sir. Just come down past the village of Broek. Any of the children on the canal will show you to our hut. They call it the idiot's cottage."

As the doctor turned to go, he muttered to himself, "It certainly sounds like a hopeless case, but I feel a closeness to that boy. His eyes are so like my poor Laurens's. No! I mustn't get soft-hearted over that young scoundrel!" And with a scowl, Dr. Boekman silently skated away.

Hans continued on to Amsterdam, elated that at last he was doing something that might help his father, and excited that he was getting the skates he truly wanted. "With Saint Nicholas Eve approaching, Gretel and I will truly have something to celebrate. If only the doctor can help father, that would be the most wonderful gift of all for mother!"

The Doctor Turned to Go.

How Perfectly They Worked.

Chapter 5

Frightening Screams

Early on that Saint Nicholas Eve, Mrs. Brinker allowed Hans and Gretel to go out skating before bedtime for Hans to try out his new skates. Once on the ice, Hans eagerly showed his sister how perfectly they worked.

Nearby, Peter van Holp and Carl Schummel were having races, with Peter beating Carl each time. Never a good sport, Carl was now looking around for someone to let his anger out on when he spotted Hans and Gretel.

"Say, boys," he called to his friends, "let's put a stop to those rag-pickers joining the race.

Hilda must have been crazy to invite them. Katrinka and Rychie are furious that they have to race against that girl Gretel. And as for the boy Hans, why I—"

"You'll what?" demanded Peter. "You'll refuse to let him skate because he's poor?"

Carl saw a look in Peter's eyes that made him back off and turn his teasing to Jacob Poot, who was skating towards them. "Here comes Fatty! And he's got someone with him, a thin fellow. Ha! They're like a strip of bacon—a streak of fat alongside a streak of lean!"

"That's Jacob's cousin, Ben Dobbs, visiting from England," said Peter. "So try to be a little more pleasant for a change!"

The boys all crowded around Jacob and Ben, who had exciting news to tell.

"We're leaving on a 50-mile skating trip to The Hague tomorrow so I can show Ben the capital of our country," said Jacob. "Would any of you like to come with us?"

"A 50 Mile Skating Trip"

"I'll go! Me too!" cried the boys eagerly.

"And we can stop at Haarlem and Leyden, and spend a day and night at The Hague," added Peter. "Ludwig and I have a married sister there. She'd be delighted to see us."

The boys made plans, then separated, each going home to celebrate Saint Nicholas Eve.

Meanwhile, Hans and Gretel were enjoying every minute on their new skates. Suddenly, a very faint scream reached Hans's ears. No one else on the canal seemed to have heard it, but Hans did and recognized the voice. He understood only too well what it meant—his mother was in trouble!

He quickly tore off his skates, crying out to his sister, "It's father! He must have frightened mother terribly for her to scream like that! We must get to her immediately!"

His Mother Was in Trouble!

Peter Was Their Captain.

Chapter 6

A Skating Adventure Begins

At eight o'clock the next morning, six boys met on the ice to begin their trip: Peter and his brother Ludwig, Jacob and Ben, and Carl and Lambert. They voted Peter their captain and gave him their money to hold.

Within half an hour, they had reached the great city of Amsterdam, a city of 95 islands separated by canals and connected by 200 bridges. The entire city was decorated for the holidays, and displays of mechanical toys, for which Holland was famous, were attracting crowds everywhere.

After a walk through the city, they headed back to the canal and skated for the next hour towards Haarlem. They sped along, weaving in and out among other skaters, iceboats, push-chairs, and strange little sleds propelled along the ice by iron sticks in the hands of the riders.

It was nearly one o'clock when the grand old city of Haarlem came into view. They had skated 17 miles that morning, but were still fresh and eager to keep going. Even though chubby Jacob longed for a nap, he managed to keep up with the others. Carl did his usual share of complaining, but he managed to keep his temper.

"Come on, boys, it's lunch time," called Peter. "Take off your skates and let's eat. We've got enough money to feed an army!"

Peter reached into his pocket . . . and turned pale. He clapped his hands to his other pockets and gasped, "It's gone! The purse with all our money is gone!"

Among the Other Skaters

"We shouldn't have let you hold all the money to begin with," complained Carl.

"We can't go on without money," said Peter, "and I don't know a soul in Haarlem to borrow from. Do any of you?"

The boys all shook their heads. Only Carl spoke up. "I know some rich people here, but my father would beat me if I borrowed one cent. He doesn't approve of borrowing!"

"How much did we lose?" asked Ludwig.

"We each put in ten guilders," answered Peter. "So it's 60 in all. I could kick myself for letting you boys down."

"So, why don't you do it!" growled Carl. "I'd enjoy watching that!"

"Let's not argue," said Jacob pleasantly. "We can go home and start again tomorrow."

"And where are we each supposed to get another ten guilders from?" snapped Carl.

"I won't let you suffer for my carelessness," said Peter. "I'll pay you all back."

Carl still wasn't satisfied and he whined,

"We Can't Go On Without Money."

"But we'd still have to go back hungry!"

"Come on now," said Peter, "let's take this like men. We can be home in two hours. Put on your skates and let's go."

The boys hadn't skated more than twenty yards when Carl grumbled, "Here's that rag-picker with the wooden skates heading this way. Must we see him everywhere we go? I suppose Peter will order us to stop and shake hands with him!"

Peter heard Carl's nasty remark and looked up to see a pale and worried Hans Brinker approaching. "Good day, Hans!" he called.

"Oh, Master Peter, is that you? How lucky it is that we meet!"

"Just listen to his impertinence!" hissed Carl. "Who does he think he is, talking to his superiors that way!"

"I'm glad to see you too," said Peter, taking Hans aside. "But you look worried."

"I *am* worried, sir," said Hans. Then he quickly smiled at Peter. "But it is *I* who can

Peter Saw Hans Approaching.

help *you* this time, sir."

"How?" asked Peter in surprise.

"By giving you *this*," said Hans as he took Peter's missing purse from his pocket.

Peter was overjoyed! "Thank you, Hans," he said. "But how did you know it was mine?"

"Yesterday, when you paid me for the white wood chain for your sister, you took your money out of this yellow leather purse."

"And where did you find it today?"

"When I got on the ice this morning, I was troubled by some problems and didn't pay attention to where I was until I stumbled against a log. Your purse was on the ice beside the log."

"Oh, yes! I pulled out a handkerchief when I sat on the log and the purse probably fell out. It would have been lost forever if it weren't for you, Hans. You must let us share our money with you as a reward." And he poured out some coins.

"No, sir," said Hans quietly. "I can't take any

"By Giving You *This*."

money I don't earn."

Peter thought to himself, "What a fine boy!" Then aloud, he asked, "May I ask what problems are worrying you so much?"

"Oh, sir, it's terribly sad! I'm heading for Leyden to find Dr. Boekman. I fear that even now I'm losing time."

"Wait!" called Peter as Hans turned to go. "We're planning to stop in Leyden on our way to The Hague. If you're going there only to deliver a message to the doctor, I can do it for you. I'm certain we'll get there by tomorrow morning and I promise to see him if he's in the city."

"Oh, sir, that would be wonderful indeed! I don't mind the trip, but I hated having to leave my mother for such a long time."

"Is she ill?" asked Peter anxiously.

"No, sir. It's my father. You probably know he's been out of his mind for ten years. Well, last night mother was kneeling before the fireplace to blow on the peat and raise the flames

"Even Now I'm Losing Time."

when father suddenly sprang at her and tried to push her into the fire, laughing madly as he was doing it.

"I was on the canal, but I heard her screams and ran to her. I couldn't loosen his hold on her, so I tried to put out the fire. But he pushed me away with his free hand, still laughing that crazy laugh.

"Mother's dress was beginning to catch fire and she was hysterical with fear. I couldn't let her burn, so I began beating Father with a stool. But the next instant, he flung me across the room, still laughing his terrible laugh.

"At that moment, Gretel had the brilliant idea of filling a bucket with his favorite food and putting it on the floor near him. When he saw it, he let go of Mother, then crawled over to the bucket and began eating.

"Mother wasn't burnt, only her dress, but she stayed up all night, putting wet cloths on Father's head to try to bring down his high fever. Oh, sir, if he were himself, he would

"Mother's Dress Was Catching Fire..."

never harm anyone or anything!"

"But why are you going for Dr. Boekman? He usually accepts only the wealthiest people as his patients. Surely there are other doctors in Amsterdam who would come."

"He *promised*, sir. He promised yesterday to come in a week, but I fear we can't wait a week. I fear father is dying. Oh, sir, please beg the doctor to come quickly. He seemed so kind when I spoke to—"

"*Kind?*" cried Peter in astonishment. "Why, even though he's brilliant, Boekman's considered the most bitter and most irritable man in Holland!"

"But his heart is kind! Please, just tell him what I've told you. I know he'll come."

"I hope so, Hans, with all my heart. Now, start for home immediately and promise me that if you need anything, you'll go to my mother. She'll be glad to help you. And please, take a few of these guilders, not as a reward, but as a gift from a friend."

"Surely There Are Other Doctors."

"No, no, sir. I can't! I'll only take money when I earn it, though I haven't had any luck finding work lately."

"Now that you mention it, Hans, my father needs help right now. He was so impressed with the carving you did on my sister's chain that he wants you to carve a door for our new summer-house. He'll pay you well."

"Oh, sir, that would be a joy! I've never carved anything as big as a door, but I know I can do it. And thank you, sir."

"Good! Then it's settled. I know you're in a hurry to return home, but why not have something to eat with us first? You've been skating for hours and must be hungry."

"Oh, thank you, sir, but I really can't delay another minute. My mother may need me. My sister is very frightened, and my father may be worse. But I do appreciate your kindness. I'll never forget it, sir."

And Hans turned homeward and sped away.

"I Know I Can Do It."

Those Long Hours

Chapter 7

Watching Over a Sick Man

While Hans was off looking for the doctor, Gretel had cleaned the cottage, brought in peat to build a fire, and melted ice so her father would have water. Then she sat beside her weary mother during those long hours.

Her father lay moaning in his bed, while her mother bathed his forehead and his lips.

"Mother, you look so tired," whispered Gretel. "You haven't closed your eyes since your dreadful ordeal at the fire last night. Please lie down and rest for a while."

Mrs. Brinker shook her head, though her eyes never left her husband's face.

"I'll watch him, mother, and I promise to wake you if he stirs."

But Gretel's pleas were in vain. Mrs. Brinker refused to leave her husband's side.

As Gretel sat staring at her father, she was troubled about her own feelings. "Is it wrong to love my mother more than I love my father?" she asked herself. "I know Hans loves him dearly and I do too, but not as much. Yet, I surely don't want him to die. I know that if this sickness lasts, Hans and I shall never skate anymore. I'll have to send my new skates back to the beautiful lady, for Hans and I won't be able to compete in the race." Tears filled her eyes and, feeling very guilty for what she considered selfish thoughts, Gretel sobbed aloud, "I'm so bad, mother! I'm so wicked!"

"Oh, my dear Gretel, you're so patient and good," said her mother. "Don't ever say such awful things about yourself!" And mother and daughter comforted each other through their tears.

Troubled by Her Feelings

Celebrating the St. Nicholas holiday

Chapter 8

From Haarlem to Leyden

Once the boys had finished their lunch and sightseeing in Haarlem, they returned to the ice and headed for Leyden. As they left the tall windmills of the city behind, they found the ice crowded with men, women, and children celebrating the Saint Nicholas holiday. Some were in the latest fashions from Paris and others in patched and ragged clothing that had seen many years of wear.

Women skated with babies tied onto their backs or with baskets of cheese or fish on their heads. One-horse sleds filled with peat or tim-

ber skimmed alongside rich women in sled-
chairs piled high with cushions and foot-
stoves, being pushed by bored servants.

Men whizzed by, puffing like locomotives on
their pipes of all shapes and sizes, while boys
and girls chased each other and hid behind the
larger skaters and sleds.

Ice-boats, from small, rough homemade ones
steered by a single boy to large, beautifully
decorated party boats manned by a crew of
sailors, flew over the ice, often barely avoiding
skaters who didn't clear out of the way quickly enough.

When it seemed as if Jacob Poot was tiring
from all the skating, Peter asked him if he'd
prefer to take an ice-boat to Leyden.

The boys agreed it might be fun, but then it
would mean giving up the adventure of skating all the way to The Hague. Still, since the
adventure was Jacob's idea and Jacob was the
one who seemed to be tiring quickly, Peter left
the decision to him.

Ice-Boats Flew Along.

Jacob sensed that the boys wanted the honor of boasting of a 50-mile skate, so he good-naturedly agreed to continue that way.

But a while later, Jacob's stout body grew heavier and heavier as his legs grew weaker and weaker until he collapsed and fell to the ice in a faint. The boys all rushed to him and rubbed his hands and feet, while a passing skater offered some wine as well.

After several minutes, Jacob opened his eyes. The color slowly returned to his face and he tried to sit up, ashamed of having passed out. The boys agreed that it was now impossible for Jacob to skate to Leyden and, secretly wishing to ride on an ice-boat anyway, they swore not to desert their friend.

Two sleek, shiny ice-boats refused to take them aboard, and they feared they'd have to carry Jacob into Leyden. But an old shabby one finally gave them a ride. This gave Jacob a chance to rest, and he was quite himself when at last they reached Leyden.

Jacob Fell to the Ice.

Stuffing Themselves on Dinner

Chapter 9

Bravery and Cowardice
at the Red Lion

The first thing the boys looked for in Leyden was an inn where they could get some dinner. They found it at the Red Lion, where they stuffed themselves on herring, sauerkraut, potato salad, and rye bread.

In between puffs on his long pipe, the fat innkeeper offered them a room for the night. "I have a beautiful large room with three beds that you should find very comfortable."

"That will be fine," said Peter. "We'll be out for a while, so please have it ready by nine."

Then, turning to the boys, he said, "Show Ben around the city while I try to find Dr. Boekman. We'll meet here later."

A blazing fire greeted the boys when they returned to the Red Lion. Seated near the fire were two shabby-looking men smoking short, stumpy pipes and drinking mugs of beer. They glanced at the well-dressed boys, then turned back to their beer.

Peter sat down at a table and explained to the boys, "The innkeeper at the Golden Eagle told me that Dr. Boekman wasn't in Leyden, but if he were to stop off here, he'd be at that inn. So I left a note for him."

After the boys talked about their sight-seeing in the city, they counted the money they had left, then decided to go up to bed.

As they passed the two men by the fire, Ludwig whispered to Carl, "I don't like the way those fellows were looking at us and at Peter's purse. They look like the pirates we saw in the museum paintings today."

Back at the Red Lion

"Pirates!" sneered Carl. "Don't be stupid! Those two are as harmless as old women!"

The boys headed upstairs, only to find themselves in a cold, cheerless room which resembled a hospital ward, with its three narrow beds in a row. At any other time, the boys would have turned up their noses at sleeping in such cold, narrow beds, but their weary bodies wanted only to sleep.

"Good night, boys!" said Peter.

"Don't anybody sneeze or you'll frighten Ludwig!" teased Carl. "He's afraid we'll be attacked by pirates. But don't worry, boys. *I'm* here and *I'm* not afraid of anything!"

A while later, when the room was quiet except for the soft snores coming from the boys, something began moving slowly and stealthily across the room. No noise came from that movement, but Peter woke up anyway. He was numb from the cold and tried to rescue the sheets, blankets, and spread that the snoring Jacob had wrapped tightly around himself. It

A Cold Cheerless Room

was then that Peter spied something crouching on the floor.

He watched in silence as that something moved nearer and nearer. The moonlight shining in through the tall windows revealed a man crawling on his hands and knees. Peter's first thought was to call out, but when the moonlight shone on a knife in the creeper's hand, he decided to remain silent.

He half-closed his eyes as if in sleep and watched as the robber laid down the knife so he could drag the clothes from the chair beside Peter's bed.

This was the moment Peter was waiting for. He sprang out of bed and leaped on the man's back, seizing the knife as he did so. The man tried to struggle, but Peter sat on him, keeping him flat on his face on the floor.

"If you move one inch," threatened Peter, "I'll plunge this knife into your neck. . . Boys! Boys! Wake up!" he shouted. "Help me!"

The boys jumped up and followed Peter's in-

Moonlight Revealed a Man.

structions. "Cut off the cord from under the mattress on one of your beds."

The robber growled and swore, but didn't dare move, since the point of the knife was at the back of his neck.

"Now tie his arms tightly behind his back and tie his feet too."

When the robber was helpless on the floor, Peter called to Jacob, "Come sit on him! You can keep him down while we get dressed."

With Jacob's weight keeping the robber from moving, Peter slid off and stood up, taking a pistol from the man's belt as he did so. "Where's Carl?" he asked.

"Did the robber kill him?" cried Ben.

Just then, they heard voices and footsteps on the stairs. Ben hurried to open the door. There stood the innkeeper, armed with a big blunderbuss. Three other inn guests stood behind him holding candles. And behind them, looking pale and frightened, was the brave, the fearless, the trembling Carl Schummel!

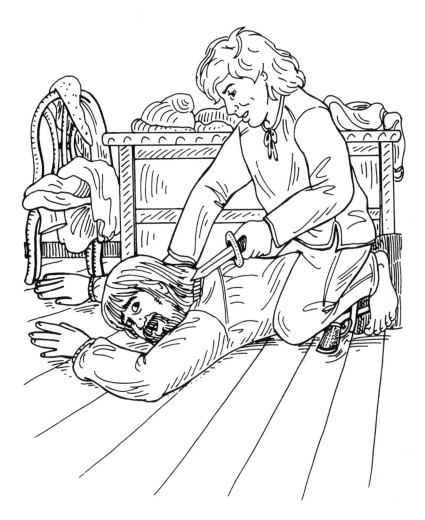

The Point of the Knife Was at His Neck.

"There's your robber," Peter said to the innkeeper. "He's tied up and quite helpless. Let's turn him over and see who he is."

Carl swaggered forward, boasting, "Lucky we caught him!"

"*We?*" sneered Lambert. "Ha! And where were you all this time, brave and fearless Carl?"

""Why-why I went to get help!"

The boys all snickered as Carl strutted into the room. Jacob stood up, and the boys turned the robber over to see his face.

"It's him, the one by the fire!" cried Ludwig. "The one that looked like a pirate."

"Yes," said Peter. "We were foolish to count our money in front of him."

"The scoundrel!" cried the innkeeper. "I'll go for the police at once."

In less than fifteen minutes, two sleepy-looking officers came and marched their prisoner to jail. In spite of all the excitement, the six exhausted boys were soon back to sleep.

Carl Swaggered Forward.

The Famous Rhine River

Chapter 10

Visiting The Hague

The following morning, the boys visited an ancient stone church in Leyden. They climbed its high wall and saw the famous Rhine River circling the old city like a moat.

That afternoon, Peter tried again to find Dr. Boekman, but didn't have any better luck than the day before. So the boys set off to cover the last thirteen miles to The Hague.

Just outside the capital, Peter cried, "At last! Now we can look forward to fine beds, warm rooms, and excellent food at my sister's home. It's just a half-mile away."

Peter hadn't exaggerated, the boys discovered when they entered the elegant home of Beatrix and Jasper van Gend, and received the heartiest of welcomes.

In a huge mirrored dining room, the boys were served caviar, meat, sausages, cheeses, salad, fruit, biscuits, and cakes, all on fine silver and china. Then servants led each boy to his own luxurious bedroom, where embroidered satin quilts lay on soft feather mattresses, rich carpets covered the floors, and silk tapestries hung on the walls.

Peter was the first up the next morning and immediately wrote a letter home, telling his mother they'd be staying an extra two days to see the city. He also asked her to send word to Hans Brinker that Dr. Boekman had not reached Leyden yet, but that a note was awaiting his arrival.

"Poor Hans seems convinced that the great surgeon will hurry to save his father once he sees the note," wrote Peter. *"But from what we*

The Van Gends' Elegant Home

know of the gruff old man, that is doubtful. It would be kinder to send a doctor from Amsterdam if Mrs. Brinker would permit it."

After breakfast, Jasper van Gend took the boys riding throughout The Hague on his fine horses, and for the rest of that day and all the next, they criss-crossed the city on foot, visiting a cannon foundry, touring the palace, admiring magnificent public buildings and private homes, and gazing in awe at the swords, clubs, daggers, and firearms at the museum.

On their final day in The Hague, Sunday, the boys went with the Van Gends to church.

Bright and early Monday morning, they thanked their hosts and were soon back on the ice, delighted to be there and impatient to return home.

For the first half-hour, they sped across the ice at speeds that caused canal guards to shout "Slow down!" They finally did, but only long enough to take a breath.

They started up again, only to face a terri-

Touring the Palace

bly strong wind coming at them. The gusts were so powerful that the boys were nearly knocked over. So they decided to stop at the small town of Voorhout for the night.

The innkeeper who served them breakfast the next morning was so astonished at their appetites, he told his wife, "Those people in Broek must starve their children!"

With the wind died down and the weather crisp, the boys set out, skating until they reached Leyden. This time, Peter had good news to report from the Golden Eagle. The doctor *had* received his note and was already on his way to the Brinkers' cottage!

Peter led the boys back through Amsterdam, and into Broek. They were all elated over their exciting adventure, but Peter was the happiest of all. He had found Dr. Boekman, and the great surgeon had, indeed, answered Hans's plea for help!

The Gusts Almost Knocked Them Down.

Dr. Boekman Explaining a Case.

Chapter 11

The Decision To Operate

At the moment that the boys were entering Broek, Dr. Boekman was standing in one corner of the Brinker cottage talking softly to Wilhelm Vollenhoven, his young assistant. He was explaining a case similar to Raff's. "My friend, Dr. von Choppem, performed an operation on the patient to remove a small sac that was pressing on the man's brain and causing these same problems."

"Did the man live?" asked Vollenhoven.

"That's not important. I think he died, but the operation was amazing!"

"And you're thinking of trying it on that poor, moaning fellow on the bed?"

"Certainly! That is, I hope to... Come here, Hans," he said, beckoning to the boy to leave his father's bedside and join him in the corner. "I'll speak to you because women often scream and faint when I discuss these matters with them." And the doctor explained the risks involved in the operation.

Hans listened attentively, glancing away only when his father began to moan again. "Did you say it might *kill* him, sir?" he whispered to the doctor, trying to maintain his dignity as his eyes filled with tears.

"It could, my boy. But I feel strongly that it will cure him, not kill him. If he goes on this way, with the thing growing larger each day and pressing more and more on his brain, he could die at any moment."

"How soon must we decide?"

"Talk with your mother now, Hans, and let her decide. My time is short. I have a great

"Come Here, Hans," He Beckoned.

many seriously ill patients to see today."

Hans went to the bed where his mother was sitting with Gretel. "I must talk to mother alone," he said, hoping to spare his sister the painful details.

Gretel gave him an angry look as he led his mother to the window and talked to her in whispers.

Meitje Brinker listened calmly, giving a quick, frightened sob only once. When Hans was finished speaking, she gave one long, agonizing look at her unconscious husband and dropped to her knees beside his bed.

Gretel looked on helplessly, first at her mother pleading with God, then at her dear brother as he stood at the window, his head also bent in prayer. Gretel knelt beside her mother and threw her arms around her.

Finally, Mrs. Brinker stood up and, in a trembling voice, asked, "Will it hurt him?"

Dr. Boekman shrugged. "I really can't say for sure, madam. Probably not."

She Dropped to Her Knees.

"And it may cure him or—"

"Yes, he might *not* survive the operation, but we hope he will. Please, you must decide quickly. Yes or no?"

Hans put his arms around his mother and pleaded, "The doctor must have an answer." The woman who had been so strong in taking care of her household for ten years now felt weak and helpless. But her son's strong arms gave her courage. "I give my consent."

With that, Dr. Boekman nodded to Vollenhoven. For the first time in the great surgeon's service, the young assistant saw tears welling up in the old man's eyes.

Gretel began to tremble as she saw the doctor open his black case and take out one sharp, shiny instrument after another. When she couldn't watch any longer, she leaped to her feet and cried, "Father didn't do anything wrong. Are they going to murder him?"

"I don't know, child!" screamed her grief-stricken mother. The usually strong, calm

Her Son's Strong Arms Gave Her Courage.

Meitje Brinker had finally lost control!

"This will never do!" snapped Dr. Boekman sternly. "The two women must leave at once!"

Gretel quickly ran into a closet, but Mrs. Brinker lifted her head defiantly. Her voice was strong and steady and determined as she stated, "I am staying with my husband! There will be no more outbursts, I promise!"

"Very well. You may sit at the side of the bed, but you must not cry or faint!"

The doctor took off his heavy coat, then filled a basin with water. As he placed it near the bed, he asked Hans, "Can I depend on you, boy?"

"You can, sir."

"I'll need you at the head of the bed."

Gretel peeked through a crack in the closet door and saw the terrible instruments being placed in the doctor's hands. "No! No!" she cried. "I can't watch this!" And she rushed frantically across the room and out the cottage door.

"I Am Staying!"

The Recess Bell

Chapter 12

Saved from Death!

The bell at school had rung for recess, and all the children hurried out onto the ice. Amid the fun and laughter, Carl called out, "What's that dark thing over there by the idiot's cottage?"

"I don't see anything," said Katrinka.

"I do," shouted Lambert. "It's a dog."

"You're seeing things! It's no dog. It's only a pile of rags," argued Jacob.

"Not rags! It's the rag-picker goose-girl sitting on the frozen ground!" taunted Carl.

The children soon lost interest in the goose-girl and skated off, all except Hilda van Gleck, who took off her skates and hurried over to where Gretel stretched out on the frozen ground, crying and moaning in a confused, almost delirious state.

"Get up, Gretel," said Hilda, shaking her. "If you lie here like this, you'll die! Wake up! *Wake up!*"

Gretel slowly opened her eyes. She had been seeing visions of angels carrying her off. But now Hilda was pulling her up, forcing her to open her eyes and to walk.

"You must stay awake, Gretel. It's too easy to fall asleep outdoors and freeze to death. You should know that. Just lean on me and I'll take you into your house to warm yourself by the fire."

"Oh, no! Not in there!" cried Gretel. "The doctor is there. He sent me away!"

Hilda didn't understand what Gretel meant, but wisely decided not to ask the frightened girl to explain. Instead, she forced her to walk

Hilda Hurried to Gretel.

up and down to get her blood flowing.

"You look better now, not so pale," Hilda said after a while. "Did the doctor send you away because your father is so ill?"

"I'm afraid he's dead," sobbed Gretel. "I can't hear him moaning any more."

"We'll go to the window and you can look in. It's not polite for me to peek in someone else's window. Maybe he's just asleep."

Gretel pressed her face against the window and told Hilda, "Father's head is bandaged. He's lying very still. Everyone is standing around the bed staring at him. I *must* go in to be with my mother. Will you come with—oh, miss! You're crying for me. How kind you are!" And she lifted Hilda's hand and covered it with grateful kisses.

"I have to go back to school now," said Hilda, giving Gretel a hug. "But I'll come again soon, I promise. Good-bye, Gretel."

Hilda smiled gently as she watched Gretel hurry into the cottage.

Gretel Pressed Her Face Against the Window.

Everyone Gasped.

Chapter 13

The Awakening

Gretel entered the house noiselessly and tip-toed to her mother's side to join the others as they stared down at the motionless man on the bed. The only sounds in the room were coming from the crackling flames in the fireplace and the doctor's deep breathing.

Suddenly, a movement on the bed, a very slight one, caused everyone to gasp. Raff Brinker's hand began twitching, then raised itself steadily to his forehead.

The hand moved across the bandage as if to question why it was there. Dr. Boekman held his breath and watched as his patient's eyes blinked, then slowly opened.

The lips trembled and a voice whispered, "Steady, men! Move that mat up against the dike! Hurry with the clay! The water's rising fast!"

Meitje Brinker bent over her husband and grabbed his hands. "Raff! Raff! Speak to me!" she cried.

"Is that you, Meitje?" he asked weakly. "I must have been asleep. Why do I hurt? . . . Why are you crying? . . . Where is little Hans?"

"Here I am, father!" shouted Hans, half-mad with joy.

"He knows us!" screamed Mrs. Brinker.

"Is the baby asleep, Meitje?"

"The baby! Oh, Gretel, that's you! He's been asleep ten years and doesn't know it. He still thinks Hans is little and you're a baby. But he's alive, children! He's alive!"

Then, beside herself with joy, she turned to Dr. Boekman and cried, "Oh, doctor, you've

"Speak to Me!" She Cried.

saved us all!"

The old doctor said nothing, but simply pointed his finger upward toward heaven. Mrs. Brinker understood. So did Hans and Gretel. And they all bowed their heads to give thanks to God.

"Why are you praying, Meitje?" asked Raff Brinker. "Is it Sunday? Do get the Bible and read from it."

Dr. Boekman nodded and said softly, "Do it. We must keep him quiet and not upset him in any way."

Mrs. Brinker went for the family Bible, but as quickly as she returned to her husband's bedside, he was sound asleep.

Dr. Boekman was putting on his coat as he explained to the family, "This is truly a remarkable case! But remember, he *must* be kept quiet. Don't give him any food today. I'll come by to see him tomorrow."

As the doctor turned to leave the cottage, Hans followed behind him. "May God bless

They All Bowed Their Heads.

you, sir!" said the sobbing, trembling boy. "I can never repay you, but if—"

"The only way you can repay me is to keep your father quiet," said the doctor crossly. "All this sobbing and sniveling will only upset him!"

Dr. Boekman climbed into his carriage, leaving Hans at the door, puzzled at the abrupt change in the great surgeon's manner. Meanwhile, at school, Hilda was being scolded severely for returning late after recess and for not paying attention to her afternoon lessons.

Actually, she had stayed near the little cottage until she heard Mrs. Brinker laugh and Hans say "Here I am, Father!" Then she knew that everything was fine for her dear friends.

"So, what does it matter if I don't recite my Latin verbs correctly!" she told herself. "I don't care one bit about them! I am so happy for Hans and Gretel!"

Hans Was Puzzled.

To Get His Strength Back

Chapter 14

The Search for Hidden Money

When Dr. Boekman visited the Brinker cottage the next day, he examined Raff, then told Meitje quietly, "He's still weak, but he needs to eat now to get his strength back. Give him red meat, white bread, and sweet wine. And put more covers on him too."

"All we have, sir, is black bread and porridge," she said. "Hans has gone to town to look for work. Perhaps when he returns—"

"I can't wait," muttered the doctor. "I have patients who need me now."

When Hans returned, he found his mother

weeping. "What's wrong? Is father worse?"

"The doctor said he must have meat and wine, and heavier covers on him. The fire is low because we're almost out of peat. And we have no money to buy any of those things."

"Father shall have everything he needs before nightfall!" said Hans firmly. "For now, give him the cover from my bed. When I come back, I'll cut down the willow tree and burn it to warm the house. I couldn't find any work in Broek, but I'll try in Amsterdam now. Don't worry, mother. We can face anything now that father is getting well!"

He kissed her, wiped away her tears, and hurried out of the house with his skates.

Once he was on the ice, Hans's confidence left him. A frown spread across his face and he told himself, "Surely the doctor knows we can't afford meat and wine. Yet if Father needs those things, I must get the money for them immediately. I could ask Master Peter. He *did* make me promise to come to him if I needed

"Father Shall Have Everything He Needs!"

help. But this would be begging, and father would be ashamed if I begged. It would be better to borrow money on the watch at a pawn shop in Amsterdam!"

With his mind made up, Hans turned back towards home. He flew into the cottage, only to find his startled mother sitting at the table, her face glowing with joy.

"Oh, Hans!" she cried. "Hilda van Gleck has brought us meat, wine, bread, and jelly. And the doctor sent wine and a fine bed and blankets for your father!"

"God bless them!" cried Hans as his eyes filled with tears.

A few hours later when Raff Brinker woke, he was feeling so much better that he insisted on sitting in front of the fire. With his wife and Hans to lean on, he made his way to the high-backed wooden chair. He sat there staring at "little Hans," who had practically carried him to the chair, at "the baby," who was now over four feet tall, and at his wife, who seemed to

Food and Blankets

have more wrinkles in her face than he remembered. Tears filled his eyes as he gazed into the faces of his loved ones.

Gretel rushed into her father's arms and whispered, "Don't cry, dear father. We're all here. We love you!"

"Yes," he said, holding her sweet young face in his hands. "But I've lost ten years of watching you grow, my dear child!"

Later, when Mrs. Brinker had fed her husband and watched him fall asleep, she sat down to eat with her children. Hans, who usually had a huge appetite, wasn't eating anything. "What's wrong, son?" she asked.

"I was thinking of all the things Father talked about remembering: the boat he was carving for me, the men on the dikes—"

"But not a word about the missing thousand guilders," his mother whispered sadly.

Then a weak voice from the bed said, "A thousand guilders! I'm sure the money's been a great help to you while I've been ill."

"I Lost Ten Years of Watching You Grow!"

Meitje jumped up. "Are you awake, Raff?"

"Yes, and I feel much better. It's a good thing we had those thousand guilders saved. Did it last you all these years?"

"I don't have—" She was about to tell him the truth when Hans shook his head.

"Remember what the doctor said, mother," he whispered. "Father must not be worried." Then aloud, Hans said, "I'm so glad you're feeling better, father."

"Yes, but tell me, Hans, how long *did* the money last? I didn't hear your mother."

"I said it was all gone!" sobbed his wife.

"Well, don't worry, my dear. I'm just glad you had it to use for yourself and the children. I'll earn more soon enough. It's lucky I told you all about burying it before the accident. I thought perhaps I didn't."

Mrs. Brinker started to rush forward, but Hans gripped her arm. Then he asked, "Do you remember *when* you buried it, father?"

"Yes. The night before the accident, I was

140

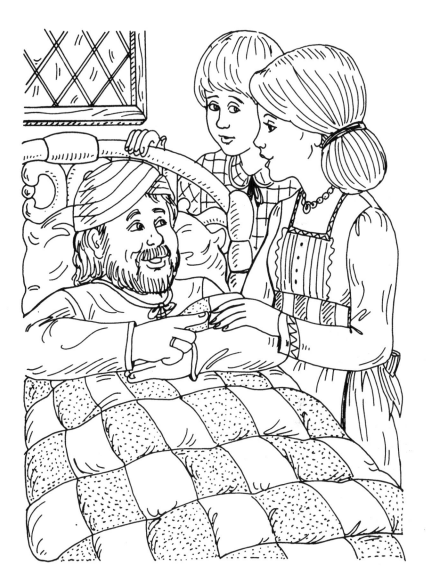

" . . . Those Thousand Guilders."

working with my friend Jan Kamphuisen. He knew about the money we had saved, but he said something that made me suspicious of him. So I got up just before daylight the following morning and buried the money. But now that you've found it, I feel foolish to have suspected him!"

Hans motioned for his mother and Gretel to stay quiet as he continued talking. "And I guess that in all this time you've surely forgotten where you buried it, Father."

"Certainly not! I buried it on the south side of the small willow tree that was growing behind the cottage. But you must know the spot well enough, my boy, for you were probably with your mother when she dug it up. But I'm getting tired, Hans. Please fix my pillows. I think I'll go back to sleep."

Hans was overjoyed! He and his mother waited until Raff and Gretel were asleep. They took an old, broken spade and a rusty ice-breaker, and headed for the back of the cottage.

"On the Side of the Willow Tree—"

The moon was full and the ground was frozen, but the two were determined to dig until they found their treasure.

They worked for hours, taking turns chopping and digging, shivering both with cold and excitement, whispering cheerfully to each other, and stopping only to check that the two in the house were still asleep.

By the time the hole was well over a foot deep, Mrs. Brinker was beginning to grow worried. "It's strange that father would put the money down so deep!" she said. "But perhaps he was wise to do it, especially since Jan Kamphuisen is in jail for robbery!"

Hans was worried too, but neither he nor his mother stopped digging until the hole was several feet deep and daylight was near. They had dug around all sides of the tree and now stared at each other hopelessly.

The hidden money was not there!

The Moon Was Full, the Ground Was Frozen.

He Spotted Annie Bouman.

Chapter 15

A Surprise Job for Hans

Hans barely had any sleep before he set off for Amsterdam that morning. He was skating on his new skates, but carrying his old wooden ones in his pocket. His face lit up when he spotted Annie Bouman coming towards him. She had been in Amsterdam for several days caring for her sick grandmother.

Annie and Hans were special friends, and both their faces brightened into wide smiles at the sight of each other.

Hans eagerly told Annie the wonderful news about his father. Since he considered her a true friend, he also felt comfortable telling her of his family's desperate need at the moment for money. He knew she wouldn't think he was complaining. But he said nothing to her about searching for the hidden money last night. "And so, Annie, I'm rushing into Amsterdam to sell my new skates and try to find a job somewhere."

"Sell your new skates! Oh, Hans, the race is only five days away and you're the best skater in Broek!"

"The race isn't that important to me right now, Annie. Whatever other skating I have to do, I can do on my old wooden ones. And now, I must go." Giving Annie one last smile, he turned and sped off.

"Wait, Hans!" she called. "Come back!"

Hans spun around and darted back to where Annie was standing.

"Hans, if you really *are* going to sell your skates, I mean really... well, I know some-body who'd be glad to buy them. You won't get

"Sell Your New Skates!"

their full price in Amsterdam anyway. *Please* give them to me and I'll bring you the money this afternoon."

"All right," said Hans as he eagerly took off his skates. "But if your friend doesn't want them, please bring them back today. I have to buy some peat and meal for my mother early tomorrow morning."

"My friend *will* want them," laughed Annie, as she took the skates and sped off. "What a brave, noble boy he is!" she thought.

And as Hans watched her graceful form disappear into the distance, he pulled the old wooden runners from his pocket and chuckled, "Bless her! Some girls are like angels!"

With the clumsy wooden runners squeaking under him, Hans made his way into Amsterdam.

But his luck in Amsterdam was only a little better than in Broek, for all he was able to earn was a few coins helping a man drive a pack of mules into the city. There was no work

"Some Girls Are Like Angels!"

in the shops, especially after the holidays, or in the factories either.

Hans had to admit now that Peter van Holp was his last resort and he'd have to convince himself that asking for help wasn't begging.

Peter was delighted to see Hans at his front door. "Ah, Hans!" he cried. "You're just the person I wanted to see. I was about to leave to go to your cottage. Come inside and warm yourself!"

Hans entered the Van Holp mansion and stood before the fire with Peter. It was there that Peter gave him some good news. "I've spoken with my father. He wants you to begin carving the doors of our summer-house right away. We have every tool you'll need."

"Thank you, Master Peter. Even though I've never learned the trade, I *think* I can do the job to your father's satisfaction."

"I *know* you can, Hans, or I wouldn't have recommended you. Now tell me, how is your father coming along? Is he any better?"

"Just the Person I Wanted to See!"

"He's improving every hour, thank you."

"His recovery is the most amazing thing I ever heard of! Gruff as he is, I guess old Boekman's a great doctor after all."

"He's more than great. He has a kind heart too. To me, medicine is the most worthy and honorable profession in the world!"

Just then, Mrs. van Holp entered the room. Peter quickly pulled a chair close to the fire for his mother as Hans turned to go.

"Wait, young man," she said to Hans. "I overheard you and my son talking about my friend, Dr. Boekman. You're right about him. He has a *very* kind heart." Then she turned to her son and said, "Peter, it's wrong to judge people only by their gruff manners."

"I meant no disrespect, mother. Yet people say he's always snarling and growling at them. Why is he so unpleasant?"

"Most people don't know the great sorrow Dr. Boekman has had. For most of his life, Gerard Boekman was one of the most pleasant

Mrs. Van Holp Entered the Room.

gentlemen I've ever known, even with his wife dying at a very young age. But many years ago, his son—his only child—disappeared. Laurens was a fine young man. He was sometimes high-spirited and impulsive, but always a good-hearted and devoted boy. The circumstances of his disappearance were painful enough to make anyone gruff!"

The boys were silent as Mrs. van Holp got up and left the room. Then Peter walked Hans to the door and said, "Now that your father is better, you'll be ready for the race."

"I won't be in it, sir," mumbled Hans with his eyes lowered.

"Not be in it! Why not?" demanded Peter.

"Because I just can't. Please, I must go."

Peter sensed that he shouldn't question Hans any further, so he stood at the door watching Hans kneel down by the canal. "That's very strange!" he muttered. "Why is Hans putting on his old wooden runners? Where are his new skates?"

"I Won't Be in It."

Laughter Filling the Air

Chapter 16

The Fairy Godmother

The sun was down, but Hans's spirits were up as he pulled the wooden runners off his shoes and trudged toward his cottage. His face brightened into a wide smile when he spotted Gretel and Annie pacing up and down in front, their arms entwined, their heads nodding, and their laughter filling the air.

"Wonderful news, girls!" Hans called out, hurrying towards them. "I found work."

"And I have good news too!" shouted Annie. "I sold your skates and here's the money." And she dropped seven coins into his hand.

"Seven guilders!" cried Hans. "Why that's three times as much as I paid for them! I must return the extra guilders!"

"You'll do no such thing, Hans Brinker! Believe me, the person who bought your skates *insisted* upon paying seven guilders."

"All right, I believe you," said Hans, who was helpless to do much else as he looked at the pretty girl with delight and affection.

Just then, Mrs. Brinker came to the door of the cottage. The girls skipped off around the back while Hans told his mother of his good luck in finding a job with the van Holp family. Then he told her how he had sold his skates and handed her the seven guilders.

"Bless you, son!" she said. "But I'm sad that you had to give up your skates. If it weren't for that thief Jan Kamphuisen digging our money from under that willow tree, we'd be rich by now!"

"We must be brave, mother," sighed Hans. "The money's gone, and father has told us all

Insisted on Seven Guilders!

he knows. Let's forget about it. I'll go find the girls."

Mrs. Brinker hurried into the cottage as Hans went around back. He found Gretel and Annie seated on the stump of a tree, their heads together in happy conversation.

Hans's smile widened as he remembered a scene like this he had once seen in a painting in a museum. "Gretel, you look just like a round, rosy cherub," he said. "And you, Annie, you're the lovely, dainty fairy."

Annie sparkled with joy at Hans's compliment. "Well then, let's imagine I'm *your* fairy godmother and I'm visiting you today to grant you one wish. What will it be?"

Hans was completely under Annie's fairy godmother spell for that moment, and he solemnly whispered, "I wish I could find something I was searching for last night."

The fairy godmother jumped up and stamped her foot three times. "You shall have your wish!" she chanted. And with more pretended

"I'm *Your* Fairy Godmother."

seriousness, she reached her hand into her apron pocket and pulled out a large glass bead. "Bury this where I stamped my foot," she said, handing the bead to Hans. "Before the moon rises, your wish will be granted."

When Gretel began to laugh merrily at this game, Annie pretended to scowl. "Naughty child!" she snapped. "You are not to laugh at a fairy godmother! For that, I shall flee from you mortals this very minute."

"Good night, fairy!" called Hans and Gretel as Annie leaped over a frozen ditch and headed towards her home.

"What a sweet and lovely person she is!" cried Gretel as she stood up and watched Annie disappear across the canal. "Just think how she spent so many days in that dark room caring for her sick grandmother!"

Hans was still under the fairy godmother's spell, and after Annie left he ran into the house to get the ice-breaker and spade he and his mother had used the night before.

"Your Wish Will Be Granted."

"What are you going to do?" asked Gretel.

"Bury my magic bead, of course!"

Gretel giggled as she sat back down on the stump. She continued to giggle as Hans began chopping away at the frozen ground.

Suddenly, Hans stopped digging and stared at the stump where his sister was sitting. Then he called out excitedly, "Mother! Come here! Come quickly!"

"Good grief!" called Mrs. Brinker as she hurried from inside the cottage. "What's wrong, Hans? Have you hurt yourself?"

In between blows with the ice-breaker, Hans cried, "Don't you see, mother? *This* is the spot—right here on the south side of the stump. Why didn't we think of it last night? *This stump* is the 'old willow tree' father was talking about. Ten years ago it *was* a tree, but we cut it down last spring because it was blocking the sun from the potatoes we were growing. That little willow tree we were digging at last night wasn't even here when

Hans Stared at the Stump.

father burying the—Wait!"

Mrs. Brinker dropped to her knees as Hans reached his hands into the broken clumps of earth and pulled up the old stone pot that had been missing from the Brinker kitchen for ten years. He thrust one hand into the pot and took out pieces of brick covering something ... a stocking and a pouch! They were both black and moldy, but still filled with *the long-lost thousand guilders!*

What a time! What laughter! What tears! Inside the cottage, Hans, Gretel, and their mother counted the coins over and over. They were amazed that their excitement didn't waken Raff, who slept peacefully nearby.

Mrs. Brinker made the children a fine dinner that night. She no longer had to save the good meat and white bread for her husband alone. Now there was money to buy whatever the little family needed.

Hans Pulled Up the Old Stone Pot.

One Last Hope—the Old Watch

Chapter 17

The Mysterious Watch

Earlier that day, Meitje Brinker had spent several hours trying to figure out a way to get money for her family. Hans had gone to Amsterdam to look for work, and Gretel was out gathering wood chips and twigs to burn in the fireplace. Mrs. Brinker had one last hope—the watch! The mysterious watch that she had been guarding for her husband all these years. "Perhaps if I show it to him now, he'll tell me how he got it and even let me sell it," she secretly hoped.

So she put the watch into her husband's

hand and stood beside his chair as he turned it over and over, and examined the black ribbon tied to it.

"I remember this," he muttered. "Poor boy! He must surely be dead by now from the way he looked when I last saw him."

"What poor boy? Who? You must tell me, Raff Brinker, after I've spent ten years guarding that watch for you!"

"Of course, my dear. I can talk about it now since he's probably dead and I wouldn't be betraying any secrets he told to me."

"Secrets? Did he steal the watch?"

"No, worse! He feared he'd be accused of murder! But I don't really believe that that wholesome, honest-looking young man could be guilty of such a c-c-crime."

"Oh, Raff, you're trembling! Does it upset you to talk about it?"

"I may still have some fever, my dear, but I'm not involved in any crime, so I can talk about what happened. It was just before dawn

He Turned It Over and Over.

on the morning before my accident. I was on the dike when this pale, frightened young man rushed up to me and grabbed my arm.

"'You look like an honest man,' he said. 'Please take me down the river a few miles. It's a matter of life and death!'

"'I'm not a boatman,' I told him.

"'There's a skiff tied up near here,' he said. 'I don't want to steal it, only borrow it for a short time. Please!'

"Well, seeing how desperate the lad was, I couldn't refuse. So I took him down river six miles, then wanted to hurry back to return the boat. Before he jumped out onto the shore, he grabbed my shoulder and sobbed, 'I know I can trust you, sir. I've done a terrible thing, though God knows I didn't intend to. A man is dead! I'm innocent, but I must flee from Holland.'"

Meitje Brinker was puzzled. "Where does the watch come into your story, Raff? You said it wasn't stolen."

"No, it wasn't. The watch had to belong to

"It's a Matter of Life and Death!"

that young man, for he had plenty of money and was dressed in fine clothes."

"Then why did he give the watch to you?"

"Just before he jumped off the boat, he handed it to me and said, 'I trust you, sir. Wait one week, then please take this to my father and tell him that his unhappy son sent it. Tell him that if he ever forgives me and wants me to come back, I'll be brave enough to face whatever punishment awaits me. Tell him to send the letter to me in—in—' That's all I can remember, Meitje. The rest is gone. Poor lad! The watch has never been sent to his father in all these years."

"Just tell me his father's name, Raff. As soon as Gretel returns, I'll take the watch to him."

Raff closed his eyes and said, "I can see the lad's face as plain as day, and I remember he opened the watch and took something out and kissed it . . . but that's all I seem to be able to remember. The rest is gone!"

"Perhaps if you rest for a while, the name

"Take This to My Father."

will come to you," suggested his wife.

Raff got up and walked to his bed by him-self, much to the surprise and delight of his wife. As he made himself comfortable, a thought came to him. "Look and see if there are any initials engraved on the watch. That might help us figure out who the lad is."

"What a wonderful idea!" cried Meitje. "Your mind is as sharp as it ever was, my husband. Sure enough! Here they are—L.J.B. We'll try to figure out who L.J.B. is tomorrow, Raff. Right now, you need to rest."

It was after Raff Brinker had fallen asleep that his wife was called out to the back of the cottage by Hans's shouts. And it was during his peaceful sleep that his family joyously counted out their long-lost treasure.

"Maybe soon the mystery of the watch will also be solved," a happy Mrs. Brinker told her children. "Maybe soon."

"Here They Are!"

The Family Studied the Watch Again.

Chapter 18

The Owner of the Watch

The next day, Hans and his mother went to Amsterdam to buy the food and supplies the family needed. Gretel was left at home with instructions from her mother to take care of her father and to clean the house so it looked brand new.

In spite of their new-found money, Meitje Brinker spent very carefully, much to Hans's surprise. Still, they returned home with food for a fine meal. It was during dinner that the family studied the watch again and discussed what the mysterious initials on it might mean and who they might belong to.

Just as they were finishing their meal, someone knocked at the door and opened it at the same time. Meitje Brinker quickly hid the watch in the pocket of her apron as Dr. Boekman stepped into the cottage.

"Oh, Doctor, c-come in," stammered Meitje. "Please excuse the house, but we were just finishing dinner. As you can see, Raff is doing well."

"Yes, yes, I see. I guess I'm not needed here, and I *am* in a hurry."

Just as Dr. Boekman turned to leave, Raff called out, "Wait a moment, doctor! I must tell you our good news, for I know you can keep a secret. Last night we found a thousand guilders that had been lost for ten years. That means we can now pay you for your services. God knows, you've earned it. Just tell my wife what your fee is and she'll gladly pay you."

"Tut! Tut!" said the doctor kindly. "I can collect money from any of my patients any time I

Dr. Boekman Stepped Into the Cottage.

choose to. I don't want yours. Hans's 'thank you' was all the fee I needed."

Meitje Brinker understood the warm feelings the doctor had towards her son, and she told the old man, "Surely you must have a son of your own to appreciate a boy like ours."

The doctor's good mood and kind smile suddenly changed into a silent scowl and he turned to the door again.

"Please don't think my wife is meddling, doctor," said Raff. "She's been very upset since yesterday about a young man whose family we need to find. You see, we have a ten-year-old message to give them from him."

"Yes, doctor," said Meitje, taking the watch from her pocket and showing it to Dr. Boekman. "It's a young man whose initials, L.J.B., are engraved on this watch."

"L.J.B.!" gasped the doctor, reaching for the watch and clutching it to his heart. "Laurens Johann Boekman! My Laurens! My son!" Within moments, tears were filling the old

"You Must Have a Son to Appreciate Ours."

man's eyes and falling down his cheeks.

Raff Brinker was finally able to deliver the ten-year-old message to the great surgeon, who sobbed like a child as he listened to every word Raff was telling him.

"Oh, Laurens! My Laurens!" he cried when the story was finished. "If only I had known sooner what happened! Is my boy now a homeless wanderer? Is he suffering or even dying while we speak?" Dr. Boekman stared hard at Raff, then pleaded, "Think, man! Where is he? Where was I to send the letter?"

Raff shook his head sadly. "That memory is gone," he sighed. "I wish I could remember."

At that moment, Hans forgot rank and position in life; he forgot that he was only a poor peasant and that Dr. Boekman was a great surgeon respected throughout the land. Hans knew only that this good-hearted man, his friend, was in deep pain. Throwing his arms around the old doctor's neck, he vowed, "I'll find your son, sir! If he's alive, he has to be

"If Only I Had Known!"

somewhere! I'll devote every day of the rest of my life to finding him! I swear it, sir!"

Dr. Boekman didn't reply, nor did he push Hans away. Then, with trembling hands, he pressed the spring to open the watch case, only to be disappointed at what he saw.

Raff explained quickly, "There *was* something else in there, sir, but the young man tore it out, kissed it, and put it in his pocket before he gave me the watch."

"It was his mother's picture," moaned the doctor. "She died when he was only ten. He hasn't forgotten her, thank God! But I won't believe he's dead, not my Laurens. Please, good people, let me tell you his story.

"Laurens was my assistant. By mistake, he prepared the wrong medicine for one of my patients. It was a deadly poison, but it was never given to the patient, for I discovered the mistake in time. Still, the man died that day while I was away caring for another very ill patient. By the time I returned the next evening, Lau-

He Opened the Watch Case.

rens was gone!" sobbed the doctor, losing control completely. "Gone! Never to hear from me all these years! Never to have his pitiful message answered! Oh, how my poor boy must have suffered!"

"How dreadful!" said Mrs. Brinker as tears filled her eyes too. "And his thinking that his mistake made him a murderer when your patient didn't even take the medicine! And all this time he's been waiting to hear—"

"Waiting to hear from this foolish man who thought his son had abandoned him!" cried Dr. Boekman. "I never dreamed that the boy had even learned of his mistake. I simply assumed that Laurens was foolish, even ungrateful, and ran away because he loved adventure more than he loved me."

"But you know now, sir," whispered Hans. "You know he was innocent and that he loved you and his dead mother. We'll find him, and you'll see him again, dear doctor."

"God bless you!" cried Dr. Boekman, seizing

"Thinking He Was a Murderer!"

Hans's hand. "I'll try to hold out hope for that." Then turning to Raff, he added, "Brinker, if you ever have the faintest gleam of memory about Laurens, please send word to me at once."

"Of course I will!"

As he turned to go, Dr. Boekman said to Meitje, "Your son's eyes are very much like my son's. The first time I met Hans, I felt as if Laurens himself was looking at me."

"I *did* notice that you were drawn to the boy," she replied with a warm smile.

Dr. Boekman's smile returned to his face as well, though it was a weak one. "I leave your house today, not only with my son's watch, but with a happiness and a hope I haven't felt for many long years," he said gently. "May God bless you, my good friends! I shall be grateful to you forever!"

"I Felt Laurens Looking at Me."

People Came from Far and Wide.

Chapter 19

The Race

The twentieth of December came at last, bringing perfect winter weather—sunshine warm enough for people to enjoy the out-of-doors, but not warm enough to melt the ice on the canals or rivers. The site selected for the race was a smooth plain of ice near Amsterdam on one arm of the Zuider Zee, the huge lake-like inlet opening into the North Sea.

The local townspeople turned out in large numbers; others came from far and wide, from every known town in Holland. It seemed that everybody, young and old, nobles and peasants, anyone who had wheels, skates, or feet had gathered for the race.

Tent-like pavilions had been set up on the edge of the ice for the special guests who had come to celebrate the birthday of Mrs. van Gleck, Hilda's mother. The van Gleck family occupied the center pavilion, with Peter's family—the van Holps and the van Gends from the Hague—in the pavilion beside them. Town officials had their pavilions, as did the musicians and the judges.

On the ice, two white columns, wrapped with greens and joined at the top with a colorful drape, marked the starting point for the skaters. Flags set into the ice a half-mile down the course marked their turning point in the race. The area between the columns and the flags was lined with a living fence of spectators.

At the starting columns, forty boys and girls were assembled for the race, chatting, laughing, gliding, darting, spinning, jumping, even

The Van Glecks' Center Pavillion

turning somersaults on the ice.

Peter, Carl, Ben, and their friends were near the starting columns. Hans was close by, wearing the very skates he had sold for seven guilders! Soon after the sale, he had come to suspect that the mysterious "friend" of Annie's who had bought them was none other than his fairy godmother herself. When he boldly accused Annie of the deed, she shyly admitted that she had used all her savings to buy the skates. Since that same fairy godmother had been responsible for Hans finding the lost treasure, he was able to buy back his skates and be in the race.

The girls' race was scheduled to go off first. Among the twenty skaters lined up were Katrinka, Hilda, Rychie, Annie, and Gretel. In a new red jacket and brown skirt, Gretel looked as elegant as any girl in the race, hardly a "goose-girl" any longer.

The crier read the rules loudly: "The girls and boys are to take turns with their races

The Boys Were at the Starting Columns.

until one girl and one boy has won two races. They are to start in a line from the columns, skate to the flags, turn, and come back to the starting point. This makes one mile for each race."

A flag was waved from the judges' stand. Mrs. van Gleck stood up and dropped a white handkerchief, alerting the bugler to give the starting signal.

Off they sped, amid cheers from the line of spectators. Katrinka took the lead for a brief time, then Hilda shot past her after the turn. Suddenly, a flash of red sped past them both to the goal, and the crier called out, "Gretel Brinker—one mile!"

The boys came racing out next. This time, cheers were mingled with laughter as a fat boy in the rear lost his balance but didn't fall. Good-naturedly accepting his last-place standing, Jacob Poot came to a halt and watched his friends speed by on their return to the starting columns.

"Gretel Brinker—One Mile!"

Ben, Peter, Carl, and Hans were neck and neck. Suddenly Peter shot ahead, then Hans shot past him. At the last minute, Carl gathered his powers and whizzed past them both to the goal.

"Carl Schummel—one mile!" announced the crier.

It was the girls' turn again, this time with the line staying close together until after the turn at the flags. Then Katrinka and Hilda took the lead, with Rychie and Gretel in the rear. Both put on a burst of speed and came close to catching up, but Hilda's lead couldn't be overtaken.

"Hilda van Gleck—one mile!" shouted the crier.

The next bugle blast sent the boys flying. Cheers and shouts from the crowd greeted Hans, Peter, and Lambert as they took the lead. Then Carl broke through, with many silent prayers in the crowd wishing that any of the boys but the insolent, unpopular Carl

"Carl Schummel—One Mile!"

would win. Those prayers were answered.

"Peter van Holp—one mile!"

The girls lined up for their third mile, nervously examining their straps and stamping to clear their runners of ice. The bugle sent them springing forward and skimming off in the distance. At the turn, Gretel took the lead and skated with a determination to win. She held the lead effortlessly, not stopping until she had passed the goal.

The crier tried to shout above the crowd's cheers, but it was no use. Everyone knew Gretel Brinker had won the Silver Skates!

Gretel's first thought was to find her parents in the crowd of standing spectators, but the other girls surrounded her and Hilda's warm hugs held her back until Hans reached her side. He was so proud of his sister, he wanted everyone to acknowledge her Queen of the Skaters!

Hans looked over to see if Peter had seen Gretel's triumph, but the normally smiling boy

A Determination to Win

looked troubled as he knelt down and worked with a knife on his skate strap.

Hans was beside him in a second, asking, "Are you having a problem, Master Peter?"

"Ah, Hans. Yes, I'm afraid my fun is over. I tried to tighten my strap by making a new hole, but my knife just about cut the strap in two."

Hans immediately pulled off his skate and handed it to Peter. "You must use my strap!"

"I certainly won't, Hans Brinker, though I thank you for offering. Get back in line, my friend, for the bugle is ready to sound."

"Sir, you just called me your friend and I'm proud of that. Take the strap quickly," pleaded Hans. "There's no time to lose. I'm not skating this time; I'm out of practice. You *must* take it!" And ignoring anything Peter attempted to say, Hans slipped his strap into Peter's skate and cried, "Now put it on and fasten it! *I* can't possibly win. The race is between you and Carl, and everyone wants to see you win."

"Are You Having a Problem?"

"You're a noble fellow, Hans!" cried Peter, giving in at last and hurrying to the line just as the handkerchief dropped.

Peter amazed the crowd with his speed, but Carl refused to be left behind with the rest of the skaters.

"Fly, Peter!" whispered Hans.

Hilda, trembling with excitement, couldn't even look up.

The cheers grew louder; the crowd was going mad! The pursuers were closing in, but—

"Peter van Holp has won! He's won the Silver Skates!" shouted the crier, joined by hundreds of voices in the crowd cheering for their favorite skater.

The music started up, and the racers, all forty of them, formed a single line. Peter, the tallest, led, followed by Hans with a borrowed strap, and the rest of the skaters. Gretel, the shortest, was at the end. The line skated as one, in time to the music, curving and doubling

"He's Won the Silver Skates!"

in and out of the arches that were held up high for them.

The procession finally came to a halt in a double semicircle in front of the van Gleck pavilion, with Peter and Gretel standing in the center, in front of the other skaters.

Mrs. van Gleck stepped down and placed the dazzling Silver Skates in Gretel's hands. The girl gasped, "Oh, how splendid! Thank you, my lady!" and made a curtsy the way her mother had taught her.

Peter received his skates, and thanked and bowed to Mrs. van Gleck as well.

Beautiful bouquets of flowers from the van Gends were then presented to the winners and runners-up, Hilda and Carl.

With a nod of gratitude to the van Glecks and the van Gends, Gretel gathered up her skates and her flowers in her apron, hugged them to her heart, and darted off the ice to find her parents in the scattering crowd.

The Procession Came to a Halt.

As If in a Dance

Chapter 20

Another Mystery Is Solved!

That night, the Brinker house was wonderfully heated with peat on the fire and gaily brightened by the beautiful Silver Skates and flowers on the table. Hans and Gretel stood by the fireplace holding hands and chatting about the race when they saw their father suddenly spring from his chair, grab his wife by the waist, and swing her around as if in a dance.

"Is he ill again?" asked Gretel fearfully. But her father's words answered her question before Hans had a chance to reply.

"I have it!" cried Raff Brinker. "I have it—

the name. It's Thomas Higgs. It came to me in a flash! Quick, Hans, write it down!"

Just then, a knock came at the door.

"It must be the doctor!" Mrs. Brinker was elated. "Fate must have brought him here at this very moment."

But when she went to open the door, she found Peter, Lambert, and Ben there instead. Lambert had a beautifully wrapped package in his hand.

"Good evening, Mrs. Brinker," said the boys, bowing.

Meitje Brinker curtsied in return and invited the boys in. "We don't have enough chairs for all of you," she apologized, "but Hans will pull up the oak chest for you to sit on. It's quite comfortable."

Once all three were seated, Peter acted as spokesman. "We were on our way to a lecture in Amsterdam and we stopped by to return Hans's skate strap."

"It wasn't necessary to go to all that trouble,

A Beautifully Wrapped Package

sir," protested Hans.

"No trouble, Hans. I could have waited for you to come to work tomorrow, but I wanted to tell you how pleased my father is with your carving. He wants the south arbor done as well, but I told him you might not have time since you were going back to school."

"Yes, both Hans and Gretel are returning to school. I insist," Raff exclaimed.

"I'm so glad of that, sir," said Peter. "Hans is such a bright boy. And I'm also glad to see you well again."

Just then, Hans quickly wrote something down in a book hanging by the fireplace.

"Yes, son," reminded his father. "Write it down. Figgs! Wiggs! Alas, it's gone again!"

"It's all right, Father. It's Higgs. I wrote it down. Perhaps the place will come to you as well." Then turning to Peter, Hans explained, "I have an important errand in Amsterdam, sir, so if you'll excuse—"

"Not tonight, Hans!" cried his mother. "Your

Going Back to School!

legs were aching after the races today. You can go in the morning."

"No!" insisted her husband. "He must go immediately! I made the promise!"

Just then, Peter took a long strap from his pocket and handed it to Hans. "I don't know how I can thank you for lending this to me, but it was a great kindness. I didn't know until I was near the goal just how much I really wanted to win the race."

Peter laughed and Hans joined in. Then Peter whispered something to Hans, who jumped back in shock, causing Peter to mutter, "All right, I'll keep them, but it's wrong. *You* really deserve them."

"Ahem!" interrupted Lambert as he placed his package on the table. "We brought this."

Peter explained, "That's the other part of my errand. Gretel ran off so quickly to find all of you, Mrs. van Gleck didn't have the chance to give her the case for her skates."

He unwrapped an elegant red leather case

"I Made the Promise!"

trimmed in silver, with silver engraving saying: FOR THE FASTEST. It was lined in velvet, and one corner had the name and address of the maker stamped on it.

Gretel thanked Peter as she lifted the case and gently stroked its smooth leather. "It's made by Mr. Birmingham," she said as she read the writing in the corner.

"Birmingham's the city in England where the case was made," explained Ben, pointing to the lettering on the case. "The maker's name, though, is in such tiny letters that I can barely read them."

"Let me try," said Peter, leaning over Gretel's shoulder. "Oh, yes, I can make it out. It's T—H—O—M—Why, it's Thomas. Yes, Thomas Higgs! See, Hans, I've deciphered—"

Peter turned to Hans, then to his parents, only to find all the Brinkers staring at him, their jaws dropped open in amazement. They all looked as if they had seen a ghost!

"Hans! Hans!" cried his mother. "Get your

FOR THE FASTEST

hat quickly! Oh, the doctor! The doctor!"

"Birmingham! Higgs!" exclaimed Hans. "We found him! We found him! I must be off!" And he grabbed his skates and ran out the door.

What could the three boys think but that the entire Brinker family had suddenly gone crazy! Peter nodded to the boys that they'd all better leave, but Raff stopped them.

"Let me explain, young masters, so you don't think this is still an idiot's cottage. Thomas Higgs is—or was—a friend. We thought he was dead, and we're hoping that this is the same man you say is in England, in Birmingham."

Ben joined in the conversation at this point, saying, "I know the man. His factory is only four miles from my home. He's a bit strange, but a serious-looking chap with magnificent eyes. He once made a beautiful writing case for me to give to my sister on her birthday. He makes all kinds of cases out of the finest leather."

"We Found Him! We Found Him!"

Raff trembled as he listened, while his wife's eyes filled with tears. Even after the three young men left, they sat, stunned, until Hans returned with Dr. Boekman. Then they told the story again and again, even though Hans had given the doctor all the details on the ride back to the Brinker cottage.

With his face beaming, Dr. Boekman listened and chuckled, then muttered, "So he's Thomas Higgs, is he? It's just like that young rascal to give himself an English name! Well, Hans, my son, I must go now, but I'm deeply grateful to you and your family."

Hans stood at the door in a daze, his eyes following Dr. Boekman as he climbed into his carriage and drove off. "*My son!* That's what he called me," Hans whispered. "He called *me*, a poor peasant boy, his *son*! The son of the greatest surgeon alive!"

They Told the Story Again and Again.

"Thomas Higgs"

Chapter 21

The Disappearance and
Reappearance of Thomas Higgs

No one in Birmingham knew who Thomas Higgs really was or where he came from, though the gossips thought his accent was Dutch. He had started as an apprentice when he arrived in the city at the age of eighteen, learned his trade quickly, was made a partner, then took over the business when the owner died.

The gossips swore that the gentleman never received mail from out of the country until "a foreign-looking letter" came one morning.

Those ladies then went on to tell everyone how "Higgs turned as white as the wall after reading the letter, rushed into his factory, talked to his foreman, hurried to his apartment, paid his rent to his landlady, and without so much as a goodbye, packed his bags and left."

Several weeks later, on a snowy January day, Laurens Johann Boekman accompanied his father on a visit to the Brinker cottage.

Raff was resting after a day of work, Gretel was sweeping the hearth, Meitje was spinning, and Hans was seated on a stool by the window, studying his lessons. All were looking forward excitedly to the visit of "Thomas Higgs" and Dr. Boekman.

As Gretel helped her mother prepare tea after their guests arrived, Mrs. Brinker whispered to her, "The young man's eyes certainly are like your brother's, just as the doctor said!"

Gretel had expected to see some kind of romantic hero who had been wandering the

A Visit to the Brinkers

earth for ten years. So she was quite disappointed at the pleasant, natural young man who was sitting before the fire. He was so different from the heroes Annie told her about in the books she had read.

But Raff was overjoyed at seeing father and son sitting side by side.

Hans, meanwhile, was thinking, "How wonderful it must be for Thomas Higgs to be his father's assistant again after all these years!"

Dr. Boekman, looking younger and brighter, was laughing as he spoke to Raff. "I'm such a happy man these days, Raff. My son is selling his factory in Birmingham this month and opening a warehouse in Amsterdam. Just think, now I can get the cases for my eyeglasses for nothing!"

Hans was startled. "A warehouse, sir? Isn't your son returning as your assistant?"

The doctor seemed to frown for a moment, then he brightened and said, "No, Hans. Laurens has had enough of that. He prefers to stay

Raff Was Overjoyed.

in the world of business rather than return to the world of medicine. But why do you look so disappointed, my boy?"

"Well, sir, to me, being a surgeon is such a noble profession. To cure the sick and crippled, to save human lives, to be able to do what you did for my father, that has to be the grandest thing on earth!" Hans gulped and he couldn't stop the tears from filling his eyes under Dr. Boekman's stern gaze.

"Surgery is an ugly business, Hans," said the doctor with a frown. "It requires great patience, self-denial, and perseverance."

"But it calls for wisdom too," protested Hans. "And reverence for God. Still, it's great and noble, not ugly, sir. Please forgive me if I'm being too bold, but I feel most strongly about what I've said."

Hans felt that he *had* been too bold when the doctor turned his back on him to speak to his son. Even Mrs. Brinker was scowling at her son for speaking up so defiantly to the

"A Noble Profession"

great surgeon.

Then Dr. Boekman turned back to Hans and asked, "How old are you, Hans Brinker?"

"Fifteen, sir," came the startled reply.

"Would you like to become a doctor?"

"Yes, sir." Hans was gasping for breath and trembling with excitement.

"If your parents were willing, would you study hard, go to the university, and in time work as a student in my office?"

"Oh, yes! Most willingly, sir!"

"And you wouldn't grow restless and change your mind just as I was preparing you to be my successor in my practice?"

"No, sir. I'd never change!"

"You can believe him, Doctor," cried Mrs. Brinker, who couldn't keep silent another minute. "Once Hans makes up his mind, nothing changes it. And he's got wonderful grades in his school studies too!"

"Then we can carry out our plan, Hans," said the doctor, smiling, "if your father agrees."

"How Old Are You, Hans Brinker?"

Raff Brinker was very proud. "If Hans wants to study medicine and you can help him, I'll be earning enough before long to pay for his—"

"Not at all!" interrupted the doctor. "If I'm taking your son away, I'm prepared to pay all costs. It will be like having two sons—a merchant and a surgeon. That would make me the happiest man in Holland! By the way, Raff, Laurens needs a trusted manager to run his warehouse in Amsterdam, and I told him you were just the man for it."

Laurens sat with Raff to discuss the new job.

Raff's eyes were shining. "I'd be robbing my family if I didn't take such a generous offer," he said. "Your father has given my son his future, and now you have given ours to my wife and me—and to our little girl as well."

The two men stood and shook hands, sealing the bonds of friendship between their families forever.

"Like Having Two Sons"

In His Grand Coach

Chapter 22

Time Passes

Time passed, bringing many changes to the Brinker family.

Hans is now the famous surgeon, Dr. Hans Brinker. He can be seen riding in his grand coach, visiting his patients or skating on the frozen canal with his sons and daughters or choosing a string of beautiful glass beads for his loving wife, Annie Bouman Brinker, who he still calls his "fairy godmother."

Just as happily married are their lifelong friends, Peter van Holp and Hilda van Gleck.

Raff and Meitje Brinker have been living a

good life in Amsterdam for many years. They have a summer-house near their old cottage in Broek, and they often are there with their children and grandchildren on pleasant summer afternoons.

As for dear, patient, little Gretel, ask Dr. Boekman and he'll tell you she's the finest singer and the loveliest woman in all Amsterdam. Ask Hans and Annie and they'll tell you she's the dearest sister ever known. Ask her husband and he'll tell you she's the brightest, sweetest wife in Holland. Ask Hilda and Peter and they'll tell you she's the kindest, most devoted friend they've ever had. Ask the poor and they'll tell you she's the most blessed person to reach out to them. And ask the van Glecks and they'll tell you the story of the darling little girl who won the SILVER SKATES.

13750